Astro-Birds

Owlkids Books

Chirp, Tweet, and Squawk loved to play in their playhouse. On this particular day, they were playing…

"Astronauts!" said Chirp.

"On a spaceship!" added Tweet.

"A spaceship called *Yellow Bird*!" shouted Squawk.

"Astronauts Chirp, Tweet, and Squawk are exploring the deepest, darkest depths of space," said Chirp.

"The deepest, darkest, most boring-est depths of space!" said Squawk. "There's nothing out there!"

"He's right," said Tweet. "It's just...empty!"

"Let's explore somewhere else then," said Chirp. "Prepare the super-hyper-speed-thrust-rocket-firers!"

"Preparing to turn on the super-hyper-speed-thrust-rocket-firers!" said Tweet.

"Wait!" said Squawk. "Before we go, I need a snack!"

"There's no time," said Tweet. "I've already started the countdown."

"There's always time for popcorn!" said Squawk.

"Buckle up, astronauts," said Chirp. "We'll be traveling super-hyper fast! In three...two...one...BLAST OFF!"

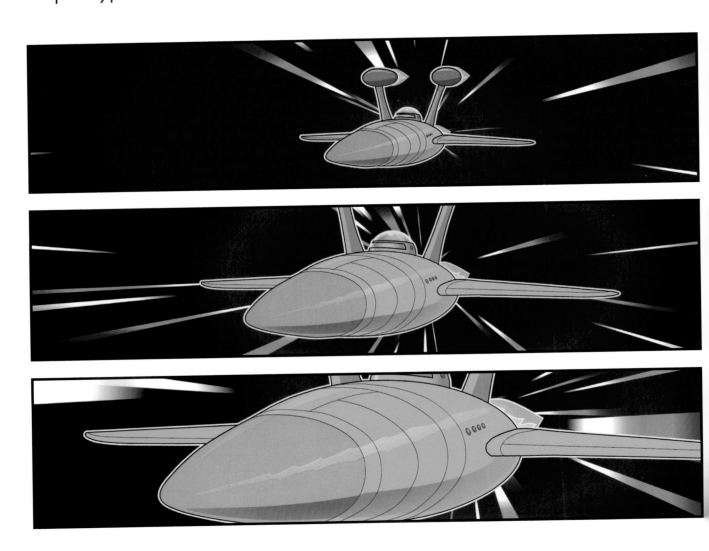

"Too fast! I don't think I like traveling at super-hyper speed!" yelled Squawk.

"Okay, turning off the super-hyper-speed-thrust-rocket-firers!" said Tweet.

"Uh-oh," said Chirp, looking out the window.

"Look at all the planets!" said Squawk.

"Those aren't planets," said Chirp. "They're asteroids!"

"We've flown into the middle of an asteroid field!" said Tweet.

"What are asteroids?" asked Squawk.

"Asteroids are huge chunks of rock flying through space," replied Tweet.

"Yikes! I think I liked it better when space was empty," said Squawk.

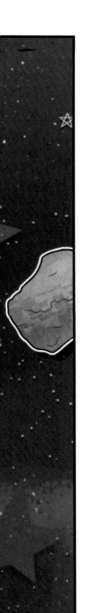

Suddenly, an asteroid hit the spaceship *Yellow Bird*!

"Quick! Abandon ship!" yelled Squawk, opening a window.

"No, Squawk!" said Chirp. "Don't open that!"

"There's no air in space," said Tweet. "If you open the window, we'll all get sucked out."

"No air in space!" shouted Squawk. "How will we breathe?"

"There's no air in space," repeated Chirp. "But there's plenty of air inside the spaceship."

"Oh, good," said Squawk. "No reason to panic."

And then another asteroid hit the spaceship *Yellow Bird*!

"There's a hole in the ship!" yelled Chirp.

"We'll be sucked out into space!" shouted Tweet.

"This is a reason to panic, right?" asked Squawk.

"We can panic," said Chirp. "Or we can look for something in the cargo container to fix the ship."

"Look in the cargo *what*?" asked Squawk.

"You know," said Chirp. "The cargo container where we keep all the helpful stuff."

"Oh! You mean the box by the front door," said Squawk.

"Quick! Let's check it out," said Tweet.

The three friends opened the lid and looked inside.

"Okay," said Chirp. "I see a flashlight, some popsicle sticks, tin foil, modeling clay..."

"What about jet packs?" asked Squawk.

"Wait, did you say modeling clay?" asked Tweet.

"We have blue, red, and yellow clay," said Chirp.

"The cool thing about clay is you can shape it any way you want," said Tweet.

"I can make a ball or a rope or even... pancakes!" said Squawk. "Okay, now I really need a snack."

"There's no time!" said Chirp. "Remember, we're about to be sucked out of the ship and into deep space!"

"Astronaut Squawk has given me an idea," said Tweet. "Quick, back to the ship!"

"Here! Help me make a clay pancake to patch up the hole!" said Tweet.

"And now we're safe!" said Chirp.

"I don't feel very safe," said Squawk, pointing out the window. "What is that?"

"That's a planetoid!" shouted Tweet. "A very large asteroid!"

"A very large asteroid that's about to hit us!" yelled Chirp.

The planetoid hit the spaceship *Yellow Bird*, hurtling the astronauts out into space.

"Hang on, Tweet!" yelled Chirp.

"I am!" shouted Tweet. "But we have to save Squawk!"

"How?" asked Chirp. "We need to find some rope!"

"Use the clay! We can roll it into a rope!" added Tweet.

"Roll faster, you guys!" yelled Squawk, floating out in space.

"We're coming, Squawk!" said Chirp, grabbing onto the clay rope.

"Gotcha!" said Tweet, grabbing onto Squawk.

"Hooray! I'm saved!" said Squawk, grabbing onto his friends.

"Time to get back to the ship and out of this asteroid field," said Chirp.

"Wait, astronauts!" said Squawk. "Before we go...I need a snack!"

From an episode of the animated TV series *Chirp*, produced by Sinking Ship (Chirp) Productions. Based on the Chirp character created by Bob Kain.

Based on the TV episode *Astro-Birds* written by Nicole Demerse. Story adaptation written by J. Torres.

Owlkids Books acknowledges the financial support of the Canada Council for the Arts, the Ontario Arts Council, the Government of Canada through the Canada Book Fund (CBF) and the Government of Ontario through the Ontario Media Development Corporation's Book Initiative for our publishing activities.

Published in Canada by
Owlkids Books Inc.
10 Lower Spadina Avenue
Toronto, ON M5V 2Z2

Library and Archives Canada Cataloguing in Publication

Torres, J., 1969-, author
    Astro-birds / adapted by J. Torres.

(Chirp ; 4)
Based on the TV program Chirp; writer of the episode Nicole Demerse.
ISBN 978-1-77147-135-0 (pbk.).--ISBN 978-1-77147-169-5 (bound)

    I. Demerse, Nicole, author II. Title.

PS8589.O6755667A87 2015   jC813'.54   C2015-901238-4

Edited by: Jennifer Stokes
Designed by: Susan Sinclair

Manufactured in Altona, MB, Canada, in March 2015, by Friesens Corporation
Job #210884

A   B   C   D   E   F

 Publisher of Chirp, chickaDEE and OWL
www.owlkidsbooks.com